To Kai and
MacaRonin

Copyright © 2018 by Isabel Quintero
Illustrations copyright © 2018 by Tom Knight

This book is being published simultaneously in hardcover by Scholastic Press.

Library of Congress Cataloging-in-Publication Data available

ISBN 978-0-545-94095-5

10 9 8 7 6 5 4 3 2 1   18 19 20 21 22

Printed in the U.S.A. 23
First printing 2018

Book design by Nina Goffi

UGLY CAT  & Pablo

AND THE MISSING BROTHER

Isabel Quintero

With illustrations by

Tom Knight

SCHOLASTIC INC.

CHAPTER ONE

O Tamarindo, Where Art Thou?

It was a rainy afternoon in the Mariposa Valley neighborhood. The gray clouds had rolled in early that morning, and lightning and thunder had been booming for the better part of the day, when Pablo arrived at Ugly Cat's house wearing a makeshift raincoat and rain boots.

He'd picked up an old lunch bag and fashioned it around his body for a raincoat, making a tiny opening for his face but covering his favorite hat. On his feet he wore something shiny and metallic and red. Red foil gum wrappers. He had used the wrappers to mold little rain boots around his feet! When he arrived at Ugly Cat's house, Ugly burst out laughing.

"**HA-HA-HA!**" Ugly Cat laughed. "**WHAT ARE YOU WEARING, PABLO? WHY DO YOU HAVE ON SUCH A RIDICULOUS OUTFIT?**"

"Ridiculous? RIDICULOUS? Humph! This, mi querido Feo, is my rain-repellant abrigo. Obviously," said Pablo. "This old lunch bag protects me, my hat, and my vest from the rain. And these gum wrappers make perfect rain boots because I can mold them to whatever shape I'd like." He posed one way and then another, showing off his rain gear.

3

As he spun around, his head disappeared into the bag, and when he popped back out, he was chewing on something.

"WHAT ARE YOU EATING, PABLO?" Ugly Cat looked confused.

"Jus a bi o samich," answered Pablo with his mouth full.

"WHAT?" asked Ugly, looking a little disgusted.

Pablo swallowed. "Just a bit of sandwich. See, Ugly, the good thing about using an old sandwich bag for a raincoat is that there is sure to be some leftover sandwich in there. Delicious."

Ugly Cat sighed and shook his head. **"YOU KNOW THAT'S A PAPER BAG, RIGHT? WATER AND PAPER DON'T MIX, PABLO."**

"Ay. Tu no sabes nada, Feo! And don't shake your head at me," said Pablo. "The cat who likes to lick sparkly things does not get to shake his head at the mouse who is eating an old sandwich."

"I GUESS YOU'RE RIGHT, PABLITO, I GUESS YOU'RE RIGHT. WHAT KIND OF SANDWICH WAS IT ANYWAY?" Ugly Cat quickly changed the subject.

"Peanut butter and jelly," said Pablo.

"MMMM, SOUNDS DELICIOUS."

"It was," said Pablo, licking some leftover peanut butter off his whiskers. "What are you doing on this porch on such a rainy day, Feo? I thought we were going to lie by the fireplace and listen to some sweet jams by Juan Gabriel, like your human Lily's parents usually put on when it's raining?"

"THAT WAS THE PLAN, BUT LiLY AND HER PARENTS LEFT FOR THE MOViES. BESiDES, I GOT TO THiNKiNG THAT I HADN'T SEEN MY BROTHER TAMARiNDO FOR A WHiLE. LiKE, WHEN WAS THE LAST TiME HE CAME BY?"

Pablo and Ugly Cat tried to remember the last time they'd seen Tamarindo.

"Was it when we thought we found another dimension but it turned out just to be your neighbor Marcos's smoky basement with all the glow-in-the-dark stickers everywhere? Wasn't Tamarindo there for that?"

"NO. THAT WAS PUNKiN. 'MEMBER?" Ugly Cat said. "HE GOT ALL SCARED WHEN MARCOS CAME iN TO LiGHT ANOTHER CANDLE. MAN, iT SMELLED LiKE CHRISTMAS TREES iN THERE. IT WAS AWESOME."

"Oh yeah. Punkin—that cat is hilarious. Maybe it was when Big Mike found that huge thing that he thought was a piece of dinosaur bone, but it turned out to be Little Jimmy's leg cast that he'd misplaced?"

"PABLO, THAT WAS PUNKIN AGAIN."

"Oh yeah. Hm. Man, Ugly, I can't remember the last time I saw your brother. It's been at least a couple weeks," said Pablo.

"WE WERE SUPPOSED TO MEET UP YES-TERDAY SO HE COULD SHOW ME THE BEST HOUSE FOR ALBÓNDIGAS IN THE NEIGH-BORHOOD, BUT HE NEVER SHOWED UP," said Ugly Cat, pacing and flicking his tail anxiously.

"Are you worried?" asked Pablo.

"NO, WHY WOULD I BE? HE'S PROBABLY BUSY," answered Ugly Cat. But Pablo got him thinking. Where *was* his hermanito? Was he okay? Ugly Cat had never gone more than a few days without seeing his brother. Suddenly, he was very worried.

"NOW I AM WORRIED. WHERE IS HE? IT'S NOT LIKE HIM TO NOT LET ME KNOW WHERE HE IS FOR SUCH A LONG TIME. OH MY GOUDA, PABLO. OH MY GOOD GOUDA." Ugly Cat's eyes widened.

"Ugly, don't overthink this—"
Pablo started, but it was too late. Ugly Cat was already overthinking.

"WHAT IF HE'S BEEN TAKEN BY A DRAGON TO A CAVE FAR, FAR AWAY?"

"No such things as dragons."

"YOU DON'T KNOW THAT FOR SURE! WHAT IF HE WENT TO THE BEACH AND A SHARK ATE HIM?"

"Don't cats hate water? Why would he go to the beach?"

"WHAT IF HE WAS PLAYING IN THE WOODS AND HE FOUND A HOUSE MADE OUT OF CANDY AND A WITCH DISGUISED AS AN OLD WOMAN LURED HIM IN AND THEN ASKED HIM TO CHECK THE OVEN AND THEN—"

"Nope. That's a fairy tale and we don't even live near the woods, just orange groves, and there are no stories of witches near orange groves. Look, Ugly, your brother—"

"OH NO, PABLO. NO, NO, NO. I KNOW WHAT HAPPENED TO HIM. MY POOR LITTLE BROTHER HAS BEEN TAKEN BY A CHANEQUE. I HEARD SOMEONE PLAYING A FLUTE AND I THOUGHT, 'MAYBE IT'S A CHANEQUE,' BUT CONVINCED MYSELF IT WAS MR. SAUNDERS PRACTICING HIS FLUTE. NOW I DOUBT THAT'S WHAT I HEARD. IT WAS CHANEQUES. HOW WILL WE EVER SAVE HIM?"

Pablo just shook his head. "Ugly. Mi querido Feo. My favorite of all the felines. My catly comrade. There are no such things as chaneques. Little creatures that play the flute and lure you away do not exist. At all."

"ARE YOU SURE?" Ugly Cat implored.

"Yes, I am sure." Pablo patted his best friend's shoulder. "Look, your brother is probably out looking for some good food. Wasn't he talking about finding the perfect apple pie? Or maybe he's just at home. I bet if we go to his house right now, he's curled up on the window ledge watching the water drip from the shingles. Listening to it softly fall on the leaves of the shrubs below. You know, relaxing."

Ugly Cat sniffled. **"YOU KNOW, YOU'RE PROBABLY RIGHT, BUT I'D FEEL A LOT BETTER IF WE WENT TO MAKE SURE."**

"All right, then, vamos a ver en donde anda tu hermano," Pablo said, adjusting his sandwich bag raincoat. He led the way to Tamarindo's house.

The two friends reached the corner of Gordita Way and Burrito Boulevard, shaking themselves dry after having splashed each other with the puddles on their walk to Tamarindo's house. They stopped abruptly when they saw a familiar-looking woman in a blue coat putting up a sign on a post. It was Victoria Aquino, Tamarindo's owner.

Victoria looked down sadly at Ugly Cat. **"You haven't seen him, either, huh, Ugly? Sorry,"** she said, and finished putting up the sign.

Ugly Cat and Pablo looked around and realized that they had walked by several posts with the same sign on it. When Ms. Aquino walked across the street, they looked up and read what it said.

MISSING

Our beloved cat, Tamarindo. He has gray fur, one green eye, and one blue eye. He loves cuddles, action movies, and cheese-flavored potato chips. Please call or email Victoria Aquino. (555) 555-5555 or tamarindovicki@mykitten.com

"Oh no," Pablo whispered. Tamarindo was indeed missing.

Ugly Cat didn't respond. When Pablo turned to his friend, he was gone. All he saw was a tabby tail rushing up Gordita Way.

GORDITA WAY

CHAPTER TWO

Lumpia, Leche Flan, and Peaches

Pablo's little feet were at full throttle as he tried to catch up to Ugly Cat. He lost sight of him as the cat turned left on Empanada Parkway. Finally, he caught up to Ugly as he was desperately trying to find a way into the Aquino house.

"Ugly!" Pablo gasped.

"PABLO, HE'S MISSING! HE'S MISSING!"
Ugly Cat's voice was panicked. Pablo had never heard his friend sound like that.

"I'm here for you, Ugly. Whatever you want to do, we'll do it. But let's try to think logically," Pablo said.

"I CAN'T! CHANEQUES TOOK MY BROTHER!" Ugly Cat exclaimed. He could see it clear as day, chaneques luring his brother to their waterfall lair with their beautiful flute music.

"MAYBE THEY WERE CARELESS AND LEFT BEHIND A FLUTE! WE COULD TRACE THEIR WHEREABOUTS IF THEY DID!"

Pablo shook his head but didn't want to argue with his friend and remind him that chaneques weren't real. Instead, he looked for a way into the house and found a doggy entrance in the back door. It was a small door for a small dog, but there was no sign of a dog anywhere.

"Feo! I found a way in!" Pablo shouted. Ugly Cat ran over, and they both hurried in without considering what would happen if there were humans at home.

Inside, they expected to hear the barking of a guard dog or a Chihuahua, both creatures to be feared. Luckily, there was neither, only the eerie sound of a hamster wheel spinning somewhere in the quiet. As the two friends made their way through the living room, they suddenly stopped, almost tripping over each other. An abundant mix of aromas smacked them in the nose. Sweet and savory. Salty and meaty. Crunchy and soupy. Food. And lots of it. They almost forgot why they were in the house. Almost.

Pablo put his hands to his face and let out an inaudible, almost-silent scream. "Argh! So much food!"

"I KNOW, PABLiTO, I SMELL iT, TOO, BUT WE ARE HERE TO LOOK FOR TAMARiNDO OR FOR CLUES AS TO WHERE HE MiGHT HAVE GONE," Ugly Cat reminded him.

"Yes...Tamarindo," Pablo said, unable to take his eyes away from the direction where all the intoxicating smells came from.

"I'm just going to take a peek," Pablo told Ugly. "Maybe there's a clue up there. I mean, look, there is a picture of Tamarindo up near that tray of...oh man... near that tray of turon."

Sure enough, next to the bananas delicately wrapped in spring roll wrappers, covered in caramelized sugar, was a photograph of Tamarindo. In the photo, Ugly Cat's brother was looking directly into the camera and sitting on the lap of a smiling kid with black hair.

TAMARINDO AND KAI

Before Pablo had a chance to say anything, Ugly Cat grabbed Pablo in his mouth and leapt onto the counter.

"Curdling cotija! Mira nomás que belleza!" Pablo yelled as soon as Ugly Cat dropped him on the counter, and he took in the sight before him. Spread out in front of them was the answer to the what-is-that-smell question. The bounty of aromas was coming from plates and trays left atop the kitchen

counter. One tray had BBQ pork skewers, another had bistek Tagalog, another had rolled-up little treasures that they easily recognized as lumpia. There were several bowls, each containing multiple varieties of fruits and vegetables, one with Ugly Cat's favorite vegetable, bok choy. But Ugly Cat could not move his eyes from the photograph. Next to the photograph the child, Kai, had left a note asking Tamarindo to please come back.

"PABLO, WE HAVE TO—" Ugly Cat didn't finish. He looked over at Pablo, who was stuffing his face with leche flan.

"REALLY, PABLO! MY BROTHER iS LOST, AND YOU ARE SHOVELiNG FLAN DOWN YOUR MOUTH! I CAN'T BELiEVE YOU."

Pablo looked at Ugly Cat shamefaced and cheeks full of dessert. "I'm sorry. It was just right there," he said, the sweet caramel sauce spilling down his chin.

"SOMETiMES I WiSH I WASN'T AN ANTi-MOUSETARIAN," Ugly Cat said.

Pablo's eyes got big.

"Ugly, you don't really mean that, do you? Come on, you'd never eat me. I'm—"

The two friends were so busy arguing that they didn't noticed that the hamster wheel had stopped spinning.

"PSSST."

"Did you hear that, Ugly?"

Ugly Cat eyed Pablo. "HEAR WHAT? I DiDN'T HEAR ANYTHiNG, AND YOU'RE TRYiNG TO CHANGE THE SUBJECT."

"No, Ugly. Listen."

"PSSST."

"There it is again!"

Their ears stood up.

"PSSST."

Ugly Cat motioned for Pablo to climb on his back, and then he jumped off the counter to find the source of the *"pssst."*

"PSSST."

"Where is that coming from?" Pablo asked out loud.

"FROM OVER HERE," answered a rough voice.

The voice sent chills up their spines.

"Where?"

"OVER HERE."

They followed the voice, not knowing where it would lead but hoping that it was somehow connected to Tamarindo.

"YOU'RE GETTING CLOSE. I CAN SMELL THE BOK CHOY ON YOU. THROUGH THE DOOR WITH THE BIG KITTY FACE ON IT."

The pair looked up at the door and took a step back. Stuck to the front of the barely cracked-open door was what seemed to be a strange, failed arts-and-craft project. It was the giant gray face of a kitten, with long black whiskers, wearing a big red bow. The face was made out of a furry material, and the gigantic googly cat eyes on it seemed to be staring right down at Ugly and Pablo. Its mouth was turned into a giant smile. It was either the cutest or creepiest door Ugly Cat and Pablo had ever gone through—they couldn't decide which, though. They looked at each other and squeezed into the dark room, searching for the source of the instructions.

"Where are you?" Pablo asked.

"UP HERE," said the rough voice.

The two looked up and saw two giant fish tanks: one with fish and one with turtles. Ugly Cat climbed up to where the voice came from. It was a dimly lit cage, filled with sawdust, and inside, eating a food pellet, was an orange-and-white hamster.

The hamster walked over to the edge of his cage, pellet in his mouth, "HEY, KIDS, I'M PEACHES." Peaches finished his pellet and looked at Ugly up and down. "YOU LOOK A LOT LIKE TAMARINDO, YOU KNOW THAT?"

Ugly Cat beamed. "YES! OF COURSE, HE'S MY BROTHER!"

"I KNOW ABOUT YOU. YOU'RE THE ONE WHO LIKES THE COCONUT PALETAS AND GLITTER. TAMARINDO IS ALWAYS TALK-ING ABOUT YOU."

Ugly Cat looked a little embarrassed. "GLITTER? HA-HA-HA. TAMARINDO MUST'VE BEEN JOKING."

"RIGHT, KID. IF YOU DON'T LIKE GLIT-TER, THEN MY NAME AIN'T PEACHES."

"Anyway, do you know where he is?" asked Pablo, who had been quietly munching on a slice of leche flan that he had brought with him.

"YES AND NO," answered Peaches cryptically.

"WHAT DO YOU MEAN, 'YES AND NO'?" asked Ugly Cat. He was getting frustrated with this smug hamster.

"WELL, I DO KNOW AND I DON'T KNOW. I KNOW THAT HE HAS A FAVORITE PLACE TO GO OFF TO WHEN HE NEEDS TO THINK ABOUT THINGS, BUT I DON'T KNOW IF THAT'S WHERE HE IS. HE'S BEEN LOOKING A LITTLE WORRIED THE LAST FEW WEEKS."

"WHERE DOES HE GO TO THINK?" Ugly Cat asked.

"YOU'RE NOT GONNA LIKE IT. AND ANY-WAY, YOU'RE PROBABLY TOO MUCH OF A SCAREDY-CAT TO GO," Peaches said.

"Scared? Why, Ugly is one of the bravest cats I know!" Pablo responded.

"SURE, HE IS. TAMARINDO TOLD ME ALL ABOUT THE ROCCO INCIDENT." Peaches snorted. "**ABOUT HOW THAT SNAKE CHASED THE FARTS OUT OF YOU.**"

"That was a misunderstanding," Pablo said. "And besides, snakes like to eat small, furry creatures. And guess what? We're small, furry creatures! We had no choice but to run as fast as we could, and if running as fast as we could meant that Ugly would be running and farting, then that's what it meant. In the end, his farts saved us!"

POOT!

PFFFT!

THHHRP!

"PABLO, IT'S OKAY," Ugly Cat interrupted.

"No, Feo, he has to know," Pablo said excitedly, his little hands flailing. "The whole world has to know that on that day, the day that Rocco escaped and chased us down the block, your hot-dog-and-cabbage farts are what saved us. Those smelly farts were so powerful they knocked out a snake and made him too sick to his stomach to continue the chase. And here we are. Alive to tell the tale, because we were saved by your butt!"

Peaches couldn't stop laughing. Finally, he wiped the tears from his eyes. **"WOW. LIFE-SAVING FARTS,"** he said. **"NOW I'VE HEARD EVERYTHING."**

Ugly Cat was getting annoyed.

CAN YOU PLEASE JUST TELL US WHERE YOU THINK TAMARINDO MIGHT BE?

"FINE, FINE, FARTY MCFARTPANTS. YOUR BROTHER LIKES TO GO TO THE OLD HERRERA HOUSE," Peaches said.

This was not what Ugly and Pablo expected. **"THE old HERRERA house?"** they said together.

"YUP," Peaches said, looking very pleased with himself. "YOU TWO THINK YOU'RE BRAVE ENOUGH TO GO THERE? YOU THINK YOU CAN GO INTO THAT GREAT UNKNOWN DARK-NESS? YOU THINK YOU CAN CONFRONT ALL THE CREAKING AND SQUEAKING AND THINGS THAT BUMP-THUMP-BUMP?" Peaches got real close to the cage and looked at the two of them.

Ugly Cat and Pablo looked wide-eyed at each other.

Pablo gulped.

"ARE YOU SURE THAT'S WHERE HE GOES TO THINK?" Ugly Cat asked.

"WHAT'S THE MATTER, MY DEAR FARTY KITTY? YOU SCARED?" Peaches asked.

"We're not scared!" squeaked Pablo. But really, neither Ugly nor Pablo was too sure of that.

"WELL, THEN, GO!" Peaches urged. "GO FIND TAMARINDO!"

The two friends stood there, feet planted to the ground.

"HA-HA-HA! GOOD LUCK, BOYS! DON'T LET THE HOUSE EAT YOU ALIVE!" Peaches cackled, backing up into the dark shadows of his cage.

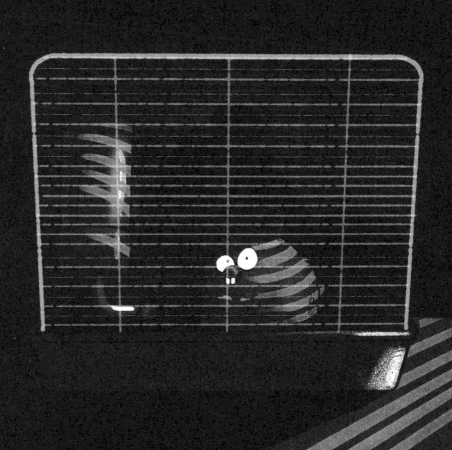

CHAPTER THREE

The Big Decision

Ugly Cat and Pablo stood in front of the cage for a while before being able to move again. They must have been there a long time because Peaches finally said, **"HEY, YOU TWO CHICKEN LIVERS HAVE BEEN HERE A LONG TIME. SERIOUSLY, YOU REALLY NEED TO GO. I NEED TO GET MY MIDAFTERNOON BEAUTY REST,"** and then he splashed water from his bowl in their faces.

"HEY!" they both said.

"GET TO GETTIN'. BEAUTY ISN'T EASY AND YOU'RE MAKING IT HARDER," Peaches snapped.

The two friends went through the door with the huge kitten and googly eyes, to the kitchen.

"What do we do?" Pablo asked as they walked toward the doggy door.

Ugly Cat stayed quiet for a moment. Then he jumped on the kitchen counter, grabbed a piece of turon, and joined Pablo back on the floor, handing his friend a small chunk of the delicious treat. **"WE GO TO THE OLD HERRERA HOUSE AND FIND MY BROTHER,"** he said.

Pablo thought about it as he ate. The old Herrera house was way out at the edge of the neighborhood, where the citrus groves began. It looked like a small ranch, with a long dirt road lined with orange trees and the bright blue house at the end of the road. It had been one of Pablo and Ugly Cat's favorite places to visit, because when the Herreras had a carne asada, they always made the best tortillas, the best elotes, the best chicken, and the best flan. The youngest Herrera, Ricardo, would always sneak food for them. He was, of course, their favorite child in the neighborhood. But then the Herreras left. They moved near Salinas, and the blue house had been empty ever since.

There were rumors that the house was haunted by the Herreras' great-great-great-grandfather. Pablo made sure to avoid the house at all costs. Shrieks and moans sometimes carried over the fence that divided the long driveway and front yard from the rest of the neighborhood.

One time, Pablo was on his way to the farmers' market to try the new pupusa place there, when he heard someone call his name. He was walking past the porch, which still had wind chimes hanging there, when he heard, **"Paaa-blooo . . . Paaablooo . . ."** It was a familiar voice, but when he turned toward where the voice was coming from, there was no one there.

"It's just my imagination," he said out loud, walking a little bit faster. Then the voice responded.

"No, Pablitooooo...it is not your imagination."

When he turned to look, he saw the curtains that the Herreras had left on the windows begin to move by themselves, and then he heard a loud thumping coming from the inside. That was enough. Pablo, ran all the way to the farmers' market. He was out of breath when he got to the new pupusa vendor.

Ugly, who had been waiting for him, said, **"WHAT'S WRONG, PABLO? YOU LOOK LIKE YOU'VE SEEN LA LLORONA!"**

"La Lloro–no! Un fantasma! Miré un fantasma, Ugly!" Pablo's voice was excited. "It was right there and I was right there. It reached out to grab me with its skinny, creepy, ghosty fingers, but then I was like, 'Not today, ghost! Not today!' and I fought it! Wham! Pow! Cawham!"

"WHAT?!" Ugly Cat shouted. **"You fought a ghost?! How is that even possible?"**

"Y luego, lo agarré de la cola, y sopatelas!" Pablo grabbed Ugly's paw and wrapped his little arms around it, as if he was trying to bring him down. "I wrestled a ghost, Ugly! I wrestled a ghost! I grabbed it and, wham, to the mat! Then I stood up and banished it back to the realm from which it came! And it went." Pablo looked very pleased with himself.

"Pablo, how did—" Ugly began.

Pablo put one little hand to cover his eyes and waved Ugly away with the other one. "Ugly, I can't talk about it anymore. It's just too fresh in my mind. But I fought it and won. Know that. Write it down. Your best friend, Pablo Martinez de los Colibri, wrestled a ghost and then banished it to another realm."

"BUT, PABLO, YOU HAVE TO TELL— WAIT A MINUTE. DIDN'T YOU SAY YOUR LAST NAME WAS GUTIÉRREZ CALDERÓN DE LA BARCA BEFORE?"

"Don't get hung up on the details, Ugly. Besides, I can't talk about it. What I need right now is a pupusa de queso. You know, to get my strength back," Pablo interrupted.

"A PUPUSA?" asked Ugly Cat.

"Maybe two. Ghost wrestling is hard work," Pablo said, sitting down on the ground dramatically.

Ugly Cat looked at Pablo and wasn't sure if he believed him.

"DO YOU THINK WE COULD GO BACK AND LOOK FOR THE GHOST ON OUR WAY HOME? I'VE ALWAYS WANTED TO MEET A GHOST."

"No!" Pablo said a little too loudly. "That's not necessary. Or probably even possible. I did banish him after all. And I don't think I should go back that way again. Not because I'm scared, of course, but because I don't want to have to wrestle a ghost again. It's not fair to the ghost."

Ugly Cat looked suspiciously at Pablo, who was looking at the sky. Ugly came to the conclusion that maybe the story Pablo was telling wasn't exactly true. Maybe Pablo just didn't want Ugly to know he was scared because he thought he'd make fun of him. Ugly didn't ask any more questions. And they hadn't gone near the Herrera house since. Just in case.

Now Ugly Cat was asking Pablo to go back to that haunted place to look for his brother. Pablo's imagination ran wild as he thought about all the haunts and creatures that could have made that house their home. He gulped. Earlier he had tried to convince Ugly that there weren't any supernatural creatures, but this was before he remembered his encounter at the Herrera house.

He thought and thought. Finally, he came to a decision. Even though he was scared out of his fur, and even though he knew there were probably one or two ghosts waiting for them at the old house, his friend needed him. So there was only one thing to do.

"Of course, Ugly. That is exactly what we are going to do. We'll go to the old Herrera house and we'll find Tamarindo," Pablo said.

CHAPTER FOUR

To Catch a Ghost

Ugly Cat gave Pablo a big hug. **"THANK YOU, PABLITO. YOU REALLY ARE THE BESTEST FRIEND THAT A BEAUTIFUL CAT COULD ASK FOR."**

"Ya, ya, ya. A ver, what's the plan?" asked Pablo, fixing his vest and hat underneath his raincoat. He was always worried that his vest would get wrinkled and his hat would get smushed; he had an image to uphold.

"THE PLAN?" Ugly Cat said as they walked out the doggy door. **"I DIDN'T THINK WE NEEDED A PLAN. I THOUGHT WE WOULD JUST GO IN AND SEE IF TAMARINDO WAS IN THERE."**

Pablo turned and looked at him. "No plan?!" he exclaimed, shaking his head. "Ugly, we need a plan. We can't just walk right into the Herrera house así no más! A ghost could be creeping around every corner, and we need to be ready. We need to be ready for anything!"

"I WOULDN'T KNOW THE FIRST THING

ABOUT A GHOST PLAN. DO WE NEED A NET?" wondered Ugly Cat.

"A net?! Ugly! We can't catch a ghost with a net! The holes are too big; it'd just wiggle its way out of there," said Pablo, wiggling his body.

"OH. I DIDN'T KNOW THAT GHOSTS WERE SO SQUIRMY," said Ugly.

"Well, know it. Ghosts are squirmy and sly. The only way to trap one is to wrestle it with your bare hands and then swing it around your head and send it flying back to whence it came!" Pablo was getting really excited.

"I THOUGHT YOU HAD BANISHED THAT GHOST AT THE HERRERA HOUSE?" asked Ugly.

"Yes! But you have to make sure it stays away," Pablo added.

"So WHAT'S THE PLAN, PABLO?"

Pablo lifted his left hand to his head and then began to scratch his belly with his right hand—a sure sign that a plan was on its way.

Pablo put his hands behind his back and sniffed the air.

"HERE IT COMES!" said Ugly Cat.

Finally, Pablo twitched his tail and clapped his hands.

"All right, Ugly, here's what we're gonna do," said Pablo as he began drawing a map in the dirt with a stick. "We'll get to the Herrera house and enter from the back door. When I heard that one ghost that one time, I heard it in the front of the house. If we go through the back, we can surprise it, instead of the other way around."

"Okay, but what if the ghost changed locations? Ghosts can do that, you know," said Big Mike, startling the two friends.

"Oh my bologna sandwich!" exclaimed Pablo, falling on his tail and clutching his chest.

"BiG MiKE! WHEN iN THE NAME OF SWEET BABY CARROTS DiD YOU GET HERE?!" said Ugly Cat.

"Sorry, kids, I didn't mean to startle you," said Big Mike, grinning. "I've been here for a bit. I was walking by when I saw Pablo rubbing his belly and knew a plan was brewing. Why do you want to go to the Herrera house anyway?"

"TAMARiNDO iS LOST, AND WE HEARD FROM A RELiABLE SOURCE THAT HE'S PROBABLY THERE," answered Ugly.

"Your brother, lost? What? Ugly, that's terrible news! How can I help?" said Big Mike.

Ugly Cat felt like the luckiest cat in the world to have two such good friends that were willing to place themselves in the clutches of a ghost in order to help him find his brother. What more could he ask for?

"THANK YOU, BIG MIKE. I HAVE A FEEL-ING WE'LL NEED THE HELP," said Ugly.

"Yes, we will," added Pablo. "Especially, if we want to send that ghost back to the deep, dark depths of Ghostville."

"WHAT DO WE DO ONCE THE GHOST IS CORNERED?" asked Ugly.

"Okay, once we do that, one of us will have to throw a wet towel at him to slow him down. Everyone knows that ghosts don't like water and they can't see through towels. Then, wet and unable to see, we can grab him and swing him far, far away! Then we just have to say, I command thee, lowly spirit, to leave this home forever!' And that should be it."

Big Mike and Ugly Cat weren't convinced.

"A wet towel, Pablo? Where are we supposed to get a wet towel from?" asked Big Mike.

Pablo hadn't thought of that. "I'm sure there must be some towels left over from the Herreras. Yeah! They probably left a beach towel or two in the pool house around the back."

"HM. MAYBE. YOU KNOW, I'M SURE THEY DiD," said Ugly Cat, trying to sound confident in his best friend's plan.

Big Mike wasn't too sure. "What if there isn't a towel there, Pablo? Then what?"

"Then we go to plan B: the pool skimmer," Pablo said.

"Nets are a terrible idea for catching ghosts," Big Mike said.

"Yeah, but pool skimmers have much smaller holes. Sheesh," said Pablo. "Everyone knows that ghosts can't fit through such small holes."

Ugly Cat and Big Mike looked at Pablo.

"Look, let's just go. We got this. Those ghosts won't know what's coming."

CHAPTER FIVE

Floors That Creak and Why Is There Quicksand Here?!

Big Mike, Ugly Cat, and Pablo walked up Horchata Street, toward the old Herrera house. Pablo knew they would have to pass Cleopatra's house on the way there and hoped that she would surely have something to say about where they were going. The three friends stopped walking when they heard a familiar whistle and the click-clack of perfectly painted nails.

The miniature Doberman pinscher walked to the edge of her yard and said, "Where are you three off to in such a hurry? And why are you wearing that hideous outfit?"

"We're going to look for Tamarindo. He's lost," Pablo said.

"And I'm wearing this outfit because it was raining and I didn't want to get all wet."

"Well, it's falling apart, Pablo," Cleo responded. It was true. The "boots" had gotten soaked and Ugly had been right—paper and water didn't mix well. His lunch bag raincoat had pretty much fallen apart, so that what was left resembled wet leaves stuck to his body.

Pablo picked off the remainder of his makeshift raincoat and the scraps that were his boots and placed them near Cleopatra's fence.

Cleopatra glared at him. "Don't worry, Cleo, I'll pick them up when we come back from the Herrera house."

"Well, I hope you don't forget them," she said. "And what's this about Tamarindo getting lost?"

"We think he's at the Herrera house. That's what this hamster named Peaches told us."

"Peaches, huh? He's pretty trustworthy. But are you sure you can handle another ghost encounter, Pablo? I heard you haven't been to the Herrera house since the day you were looking for the perfect pupusa but got the chili fries scared out of you instead."

Pablo said, 'I'm not scared, Cleopatra. And I didn't get the chili fries scared out of me. I dropped them when I was running—Wait. How did you know I was eating chili fries that day? I hadn't even told Ugly that part."

Cleopatra smiled mischievously. "Bye, Pablo. Hope to see you again real soon," she said as she turned to walk back to her porch.

"YOU HAD CHILI FRIES WITHOUT ME, PABLO? THAT'S MESSED UP. IF WE WEREN'T ON OUR WAY TO FIND MY BROTHER, I DON'T KNOW IF I'D EVEN BE

TALKING TO YOU RIGHT NOW. YOU KNOW HOW I FEEL ABOUT CHILI FRIES," said Ugly Cat.

"I'm sorry, Ugly, I just happened to come across some that
day and couldn't pass them up.
But that's in the past. Right now,
we have to find your brother,"
Pablo responded.

"Oh! What a surprise!" Cleopatra said, quickly
turning back to face them. "Pablo just happened
to find some food that's unattended."

"Not the elote thing again. I
told you I was sorry about that,
Cleo."

"Yeah, Pablo, you did. I still don't think it was an accident. I think you saw me about to eat my elote, were jealous you didn't have one, and took your chance the minute I walked away. One minute! That's all it took for you to pounce on my corn!"

Pablo put his head in his hands and shook his head. "For the last time, Cleo, I didn't steal it. I didn't know it was yours! It was just lying on the ground! How was I supposed to know it belonged to you? And if you wanted it so bad, why did you walk away? Who abandons an elote?"

"Ha! Just lying on the ground? Why would I leave my elote just lying on the ground, Pablo? Why?" Cleopatra got close to the fence. "It was on a plate. Near my food bowl. Leonidas, my human, bought it for me. He even got me extra cheese. Extra cheese, Pablo!"

Pablo stepped up to the fence, too. "Well, I cannot imagine why anyone would leave an elote unattended like that. And you know what, I am soooo happy I ate it! It was delicious!

Mm-mm-mm!" Pablo rubbed his belly and licked his lips.

Cleo gasped. "I knew it! I knew it! You ate it on purpose! I had been dreaming about the little kernels smothered in mayonesa, butter, chili powder, and cheese, when from a distance I see this gray goblin hunched over my corn just munching away. I cannot believe you, Pablo! This, this . . . ahhhhhh!"

"**ENOUGH TALK ABOUT THE DUMB CORN!**" Ugly exclaimed. "**I NEED TO FIND MY BROTHER. THAT'S WHAT'S IMPORTANT NOW. PABLO, WE HAVE TO GO.**"

"Argh! You're right. I'm sorry, Ugly," said Pablo. "Look, Cleo, I didn't eat it on purpose, but I can't talk about this right now because I have more pressing matters. We can talk about it later."

Cleo glared at Pablo.

Big Mike had been nervously watching the exchange. He didn't want to get in the middle of the Pablo-Cleo feud. "Bye, Cleopatra," he said quietly.

"Bye, Big Mike. Bye, ugly. Good luck finding your brother," Cleo said as the three friends walked away.

Pablo was still upset when they reached the Herrera house. The whole walk there he had been going on about how he couldn't believe Cleo. Finally, Big Mike said, "Pablo, right now we have to worry about Tamarindo. No elote is more important than your best friend's brother."

Pablo realized he had been talking only about himself. "You're right. I'm sorry, Ugly. Let's go find your brother," Pablo said as they walked up to the gate outside the giant house.

The grass in the front yard was overgrown, and wildflowers had begun to take over. As they crossed the yard, only Ugly Cat's and Big Mike's scraggly and stumpy tails could be seen swishing and wagging as they walked. However, Pablo's small body was completely hidden by the grass. His nose caught a whiff of something stinky.

"Queso de rancho," Pablo whispered as he got distracted again. He walked a few steps and found an old piece of cheese lying on the ground. He picked it up, gave it a nibble, and put it under his hat for later. Then there was a breeze, and something brushed against his tail.

"Ahhh! Ghost!" Pablo screamed.

Big Mike looked over at him and shook his head. "That's not a ghost, Pablo, that's just a dandelion puff. Sheesh," he said. "Stop being such a gallina."

Pablo cautiously continued down the path toward the front of the house.

When they finally reached the door, they heard loud thumps come from inside.

"Did you hear that?!" Pablo whispered loudly.

"No," Big Mike said timidly.

Suddenly, they heard quick footsteps from inside the house.

"Oh my Gouda!" Pablo yelled.

"Okay, sorry guys, but I...I...I can't fight a ghost...!" Big Mike screamed as he ran back to the street through the tall grass, his little tail wiggling behind him.

Ugly Cat shook his head. **"AND THAT GUY CALLED YOU A CHICKEN."**

"Are we really going in, Ugly?"
Pablo asked, his voice shaking.

**"WHAT OTHER CHOICE DO WE HAVE?
LET'S GO,"** Ugly said as he softly pushed the
door with his paw.

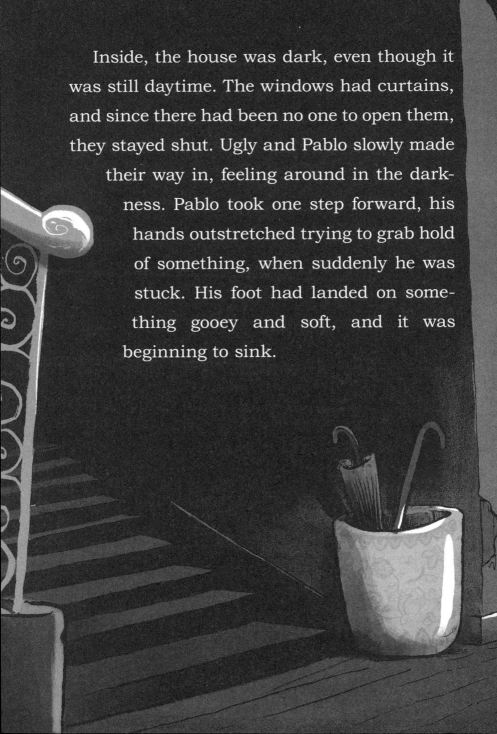

Inside, the house was dark, even though it was still daytime. The windows had curtains, and since there had been no one to open them, they stayed shut. Ugly and Pablo slowly made their way in, feeling around in the darkness. Pablo took one step forward, his hands outstretched trying to grab hold of something, when suddenly he was stuck. His foot had landed on something gooey and soft, and it was beginning to sink.

"Ugly! I think I stepped in quicksand!" Pablo exclaimed. His voice was panicked. He had seen quicksand in cartoons, so he knew that Ugly Cat would need some sort of tree branch to help pull him out and there weren't any trees around.

"QUICKSAND? WHY WOULD THERE BE QUICKSAND IN HERE?" Ugly Cat asked.

Ugly Cat, who could see in the dark because he was a cat and all cats can see in the dark, looked down at Pablo's predicament and tried not to laugh.

"OH, PABLITO, THAT IS DEFINITELY NOT QUICKSAND. YOU STEPPED IN SOME- ONE'S OLD GUM." Ugly Cat stuck his tongue out and licked the gooey blob. **"YEP, IT'S GUM, ALL RIGHT. IT'S A MIX BETWEEN SOMETHING FRUITY AND SOMETHING MINTY."** He gave another lick and said, **"I DON'T KNOW WHY SOMEONE WOULD SPIT OUT PERFECTLY GOOD GUM."**

Pablo stared at Ugly Cat with disgust. "I can't believe you just licked already-chewed gum, Ugly! Qué te pasa? Seriously, what is wrong with you? That is so gross!"

"I KNOW IT'S GROSS, PABLO! BUT I CAN'T HELP IT. YOU SHOULD KNOW THAT BY NOW—WE'VE BEEN BEST FRIENDS FOR A WHILE. IF I SEE SOMETHING KIND OF SHINY ON THE FLOOR, LIKE THIS PIECE OF GUM, I'M GONNA LICK IT. I JUST CAN'T HELP MYSELF. IT'S LIKE SHINY THINGS CALL TO ME: 'UGLY ... UGLY ... YOU KNOW YOU WANT TO TASTE US ... WE ARE SO VERY DELICIOUS ... UGLY, COME CLOSER ... JUST A LITTLE LICK,' AND THEN I HAVE TO."

Pablo shook his head. "Ugly, Ugly, Ugly. You are one strange gato. Can you please take a break from licking an old piece of gum and help me out of here?"

The two friends tried to figure out a way of rescuing Pablo's foot from the gum, but they only made it worse.

"Ouch!" Pablo screamed. "When you pull my foot, the little hairs are pulled, too! You know how much I love my hairy feet! Be careful with these beauties."

Ugly Cat rolled his eyes. He thought Pablo couldn't see him in the dark.

"And don't roll your eyes at me. You know I have beautiful feet. Think. Let's try to figure this out," Pablo said.

"I HAVE A SOLUTION. BUT YOU'RE NOT GOING TO LIKE IT."

"What is it, Ugly?"

"SERIOUSLY, PABLO. YOU'RE NOT GOING TO LIKE IT."

"Ugly, we have to go look for your brother. We have no time for games." Pablo was getting impatient. He began imagining his foot being stuck in the piece of gum forever. Which meant he'd be in the Herrera house forever. It was too much. Little drops of sweat were beginning to form on his forehead.

"UGLY! What's the plan? I can't be stuck in this piece of gum forever!"

"OKAY. I THINK IF I LICK YOUR FOOT AND BETWEEN YOUR TOES, I CAN LOOSEN YOUR FOOT."

A strange gurgling sound came from Pablo's throat. "Arghrgh, so gross. So gross. But if it will save me from being stuck here forever, then you must do it.

"Let me know when you're going to do it, Ugly. It's dark and I can't see you, and I don't want to be surprised."

"OKAY, PABLO."

"Mira, Feo, I'm serious. Don't you dare do it without telling me."

"YES, PABLO. DON'T GET YOUR CHONIES IN A BUNCH. I'M BENDING DOWN—"

"Ugly, I can smell your tuna breath. You better not surprise-uuuugggh. Ugly! I told you to tell me!"

Ugly Cat could not stop laughing, and because he was trying to lick Pablo's foot at the same time, he accidentally licked Pablo's face and head, too.

"PABLO, HA-HA-HA! OH, PABLO, YOUR FACE!" Ugly Cat kept on laughing. He was on his back laughing, rolling around on the dirty floor. Tears were streaming down; he was laughing so hard. **"YOUR FACE WAS PRICELESS."**

He tasted something salty and spit it out.
"WHAT THE . . . PABLO, WHEN I LICKED YOUR HEAD, I ACCIDENTALLY ALMOST ATE YOUR HAT!" He started laughing again. **"WHEN DID YOU START HIDING CHEESE UNDER THERE?"**

Pablo was furious. "Give me my hat."

"PABLO, YOU DON'T WANT IT."

"Give. Me. My. Hat."

"OKAY, OKAY. BUT DON'T SAY I DIDN'T WARN YOU THAT YOUR HAT WAS FILLED WITH BABA."

Pablo grabbed his cap back and immediately regretted it. He'd have to take a bath now.

"UGLY CAT!!! My foot, it's still stuck!" Pablo pulled at his leg, unable to move it. "Ugly, help me. If I can't move my leg, we can't look for your brother. It is in your best-"

Pablo couldn't finish his sentence because just then they heard screaming.

The thumping on the second floor got thumpier.

Thump, thump, thump. Thump, thump, thump.

"RUUUUUN! RUUUUUUN!"

CHAPTER SIX

The Sounds Revealed

Ugly Cat couldn't see where the voices were coming from, but then he felt something crawling on his paws. Cockroaches. Dozens of them. Running away from something as fast as their six little feet could carry them.

"What's happening, Ugly?" Pablo was scared.

"MILLIONS OF CUCARACHITAS ARE RUNNING EVERYWHERE!" Ugly said.

The thumping from the second floor got louder.

THUMPTHUMPTHUMPTHUMPTHUMP.

"OH NO! OH NO! SOMETHING IS COMING! COME ON, PABLO!" Ugly Cat yelled.

"My foot is still stuck! I can't move it! Ugly, what do I do?" Pablo implored.

THUMPTHUMPTHUMPTHUMPTHUMP.

"I'M SORRY, FRIEND. I REALLY AM," Ugly said to Pablo. **"THIS IS GONNA HURT."** The cat pulled Pablo as hard as he could.

"AAHHH!" screamed Pablo. "I think I lost half my fur, Feo. Oh, I'm dizzy. So dizzy. I think I'm gonna faint."

"KEEP IT TOGETHER, PABLO, WE HAVE TO RUN!"

"Good night, Ugly. Nice knowing you," Pablo said as he wobbled around in the dark.

Ugly picked him up with his teeth and took off after the cockroaches, which had scurried under a closet door. The door had been left ajar, and Ugly squeezed himself in, Pablo dangling from his mouth.

"Hey! What's this? A cat with a snack? No, no, sir. This here is our hiding place!" one of the cockroaches told Ugly.

"WHAT?! A SNACK?! NO! THIS IS MY BEST FRIEND; HE JUST PASSED OUT BECAUSE—IT DOESN'T MATTER! JUST PLEASE, LET US STAY. WHATEVER IS OUT THERE IS GETTING CLOSER," Ugly whispered as loud steps bounded down the stairs.

"Fine," said the cockroach. "But keep it quiet."

As the footsteps got closer, voices came with them. Strange voices making horrible screeching sounds. Ugly and the cockroaches held their breaths.

"OH, I CAN'T STAND IT! I CAN'T STAND IT!" Ugly began to panic. The strange screeching got closer. Then it stopped.

"I wonder what's in here, you guys?" the voice said. The screeching began again as the knob on the door turned.

"Wait, is that singing?" one of the cockroaches asked.

"I think so," answered another one.

The door opened, and the closet was flooded
with light from the flashlight in the hands of a
singing teenager. All the creatures in the closet
were stunned. Pablo immediately woke up,
saw the light, and screamed, "Aliens!" con-
fusing the light from the flashlight as a beam
from a UFO.

Ugly let out a loud hiss, and a very surprised teenage boy shrieked and tossed the flashlight. He was not expecting to see a cat, a mouse with a vest and hat, and dozens of cockroaches huddled together.

"Attack!" The cockroaches charged.

"Killer cucarachas! There's millions of them!" the boy shouted at his friends, who screamed and took off out the back and front doors, throwing the potato chips and Pop Rocks they had been eating everywhere.

When all the commotion had settled down, the cockroaches walked back to the closet where Ugly Cat and Pablo were still hiding.

"What happened?" Pablo asked. "And why am I missing hair on my foot? Oh, wait, I remember, the gum! I was stuck in gum and you yanked me out, and my poor little hairs came out!" Pablo cried.

"PABLO, ONLY LIKE FIVE HAIRS CAME OUT OF YOUR FOOT," Ugly responded. "I NEEDED TO DO IT BECAUSE I THOUGHT YOUR LIFE WAS IN DANGER. WOULD YOU RATHER I HAD LEFT YOU THERE, STUCK IN A PIECE OF CHEWED CHICLE?"

"Obviously not, Ugly. It's just that my foot is hideous now. Look at it! Look at it!" Pablo exclaimed.

Ugly and the cockroaches looked at his foot.

"Dude. Your foot looks totally rad. It's like the coolest and hairiest mouse foot I've ever seen," said the cockroach who seemed to possess the aura of a leader, patting Pablo on the back and giving him a thumbs-up.

"Thank you, but I know you're just being kind," Pablo said, milking the attention.

"JEEZ LOUISE, PABLO. TE DIGO. YOU'LL BE GROWING HAIR AGAIN SOON. IT'S NOT PERMANENT," Ugly said.

"You're right. You're right, Ugly, my foot will be back to its furry self in no time. Now, let's find your brother," Pablo said.

"HEY, MAYBE YOU GUYS HAVE SEEN HIM." Ugly turned to the cockroaches. "HAVE Y'ALL LIVED HERE A WHILE? MY BROTHER TAMARINDO IS LOST AND I AM TRYING TO FIND HIM."

"A lost kitty cat? Hmm. Well, we have seen one who looks a

bit like you, but bigger. He's come by a few times. Looking a bit anxious. Don't know what kinda trouble he's mixed up in. I'm Lenny, by the way," said the lead cockroach.

"Nice to meet you, Lenny. I'm Pablo, and this is Ugly Cat. Ugly for short, and Feo to those close to him," said Pablo.

"MY BROTHER WOULDN'T BE MiXED UP iN ANY TROUBLE—HE'S A GOOD CAT. DOESN'T EVEN COUGH HAiR BALLS iN FRONT OF PEOPLE," Ugly Cat said. He was very defensive about his brother. "AND MAYBE HE WAS iN TROUBLE, BUT NOT MiXED UP iN iT."

"Maybe," said Lenny.

"When was the last time you saw him around here?" asked Pablo.

"Ay, George, when did we see that cat who looks like this cat but bigger?" Lenny said, pointing at Ugly. "Yesterday? Remember by the bushes? I thought it was a rabbit and you were like, 'That's not a rabbit, that's a cat.' It was yesterday, right?"

"You and those rabbits! Yes, it was yesterday. But I saw him today as well," said George.

Then his voice got quieter and more mysterious as he stepped into a shadow. "In fact, he was in that very closet where we were hiding. Just sitting there, pretty as you please."

"**WHAT?!**" said Ugly. "**HE WAS iN THAT CLOSET? MAYBE THERE ARE CLUES iN THERE!**" Ugly Cat looked inside the closet.

"**OH NO!**" he groaned. "**THiS iS BAD.**" He walked out of the closet with something shiny in his teeth.

"Oh no. This *is* bad," echoed Pablo. "That's Tamarindo's favorite collar. He would never leave it behind."

"**UNLESS SOMETHING TRAGIC HAP-PENED,**" added Ugly Cat, his imagination starting to go wild. "**CHANEQUES! I TOLD YOU, PABLO. THEY WOULD COME FOR HiM!**"

"What in the world are chaneques?" asked Lenny.

"They're mythological creatures, like little trolls, that play their flutes and lure people into their lair. They're not real, but Ugly insists they are," Pablo explained. "This is not the work of chaneques, Feo."

"Flutes, huh?" said George getting closer and closer to Ugly Cat's face. The other cockroaches started talking nervously among themselves. "That lure you to their lair?"

Ugly Cat's eyes widened. **"YES, TO THEIR LAIR. WHY?"**

Lenny nervously asked, "This lair, it wouldn't be near water, would it?"

Pablo gulped. "It's always near water. Why?"

"Well," George started off, "we've seen your brother and we've heard the flutes. The flutes have been coming from a small waterfall outside. But we haven't seen your brother since the flutes stopped playing."

"Wait," Pablo jumped in, "if you heard the flutes, then why didn't you get lured to their lair?"

Lenny answered smugly, **"Because cockroaches can't be tricked so easily. We're smarter than that."**

"Whaaaaaat," said Pablo. "Are you insinuating something?"

"GUYS! WE DON'T HAVE TIME FOR THIS!" Ugly Cat was frustrated. **"JUST, PLEASE, TELL US, WHERE IS THE LAIR?"**

"The lair is out–" George wasn't able to finish his sentence because just then the quiet whistling of a flute could be heard coming from the other side of the back door. The one the teenagers had left slightly open.

CHAPTER SEVEN

El Ojo de Agua

Ugly began walking toward the door, his body swaying to the rhythm of the music as he walked.

"Ugly, where are you going?" Pablo asked, but Ugly didn't respond.

"Dude, come back!" shouted Lenny.

"BUT IT SOUNDS SO BEAUTIFUL," said Ugly Cat. "I WANT TO SEE WHERE IT'S COMING FROM."

"Chaneques," Pablo said under his breath. He couldn't believe it. There really were chaneques. What else would be playing that music?

"We have to go after him," said Pablo to the rest of the group.

"Yeah, about that . . ." George said. "I don't think we can."

"But we'll definitely send good thoughts your way," added Lenny.

"What?! Y'all are wimps!" Pablo exclaimed.

"Come on, man. I wouldn't call us wimps. We're simply cautious," responded George.

"Argh. Wimps!" Pablo cried out to the heavens, shaking his little fists.

"That's okay, Pablito, I'm here for you," said a booming voice.

"Ah! Sweet and spicy pickles, it's a ghost!" Pablo clutched his chest.

"No, Pablo, it's not a ghost. It's me," answered Big Mike.

"Big Mike! I thought you were too scared to come in?"

"I was, but then I got to feeling guilty and couldn't leave you all by yourself," he said.

"Well, thank you, amigo, it means a lot to us. But let's stop wasting time; we need to help Ugly!" said Pablo anxiously.

Big Mike and Pablo took after Ugly, who was still walking to the rhythm of the flute music when they caught up to him outside. Pablo grabbed Ugly by the tail, but Ugly just flicked his tail hard and sent Pablo flying.

"SORRY, PABLO, BUT I HAVE TO FOLLOW THE MUSIC," said Ugly.

Pablo stood up and dusted himself off. Big Mike went over to him and tried to help but Pablo wasn't having it.

"Ugh! I'm fine, Big Mike. Just fine," Pablo said, annoyed when Big Mike tried to lick him clean. "I said I'm fine! Sheesh. We can't let Ugly out of

our sight!" With that, the two hurried after Ugly once more so as not to lose him.

Ugly followed the flute music to what seemed like an old waterfall. In reality, it was a fake waterfall cascading over the grotto that the Herreras had built. It was strange because the house was abandoned and the pool shouldn't have been on at all. Yet the water was flowing and the pool was clean. The music came from the grotto, which had a huge mosaic of an eye on the wall.

"Un ojo de agua," said Pablo. He was in awe that the chaneque legend seemed to be true. Here they were at un ojo de agua, a water hole, or water's eye, just like the legend said. From where Pablo and Big Mike were standing, they could make out Ugly Cat's orange body on the other side of the waterfall, in front of the giant eye. They ran to him.

But whoever thought to clean the pool didn't think to put new lights in the grotto, and so Pablo and Big Mike were walking into a shadowy place. It was still raining, and the gray sky loomed over them. The raindrops made eerie echoing sounds in the silent backyard. All around them were orange groves, and it smelled like orange blossoms and wet dirt. Pablo and Big Mike walked into the grotto closely together.

"Oh my Gouda, Big Mike," Pablo loud whispered. "What is this?"

Flute music got louder the more they walked in.

"I—I—I don't know, Pa-Pa-Pablo," Big Mike shivered with fear.

When Pablo and Big Mike got to the wall where Ugly Cat had disappeared, the music stopped.

"Oh man," said Big Mike, "I can't move my legs."

"You're going to have to try," said Pablo.

"Dude, I can't." Big Mike was petrified.

"Oh, yes, you can!" said Pablo, giving Big Mike one big push.

They finally saw what was around the corner, and both let out one big scream, clutching their faces.

CHAPTER EIGHT

Tamarindo at Last!

"AND MORE IMPORTANT, WHY ARE YOU FARTING?!" asked Ugly Cat, holding his nose.

"I don't know!" said Pablo, clutching his chest and breathing heavily. "I'm a little dizzy. I need to sit down."

"I guess we didn't know what we would find here, so we screamed and farted preemptively, you know, attacking before we were attacked?" said Big Mike.

"WOW, YOU GUYS ARE SOMETHING ELSE," said Tamarindo. "YOUR FARTS WOKE UP THE KIDS."

"THE KIDS?!" Big Mike and Pablo said together.

"YES, THE KIDS," said Tamarindo. "I NEED TO MAKE SURE THEY DIDN'T PASS OUT FROM THAT TORTA DE HUEVO FART YOU LET LOOSE."

Big Mike got a little embarrassed. "Sheesh, Tamarindo. You didn't have to say it was me."

Everyone looked at Big Mike. **"WE all KNEW iT was YOU."**

Pablo reassured his friend. "It's okay, Big Mike. Everybody farts." He patted Big Mike on the back. "Just not like that," he added under his breath.

"Hey! I heard that!" said Big Mike.

Pablo gave him a big cheesy grin.

Ugly Cat was anxious for answers and bombarded Tamarindo with questions. **"I HAVE SO MANY QUESTIONS! WHERE HAVE YOU BEEN, TAMARINDO? WE'VE BEEN SO WORRIED! WHAT KIDS ARE YOU TALKING ABOUT? AND THE FLUTE MUSIC? WHERE DID THAT GO?"**

Tamarindo sighed and smiled. **"WELL, I WASN'T LOST. I WAS JUST HELPING COUSIN TERE WITH HER NEW KITTENS."** Tamarindo pointed to a corner where, up until now, Pablo hadn't noticed another tabby cat, Tere. Next to her were three little kittens, squirming around.

"DARLIN'?" said Ugly Cat. **"SINCE WHEN DO YOU SAY 'DARLIN'' AND SINCE WHEN DO YOU HAVE A SOUTHERN ACCENT?"**

"Never you mind, Ugly," Pablo retorted as he ran toward the kittens.

"Mama, is that lunch?" asked one of the kittens, stopping Pablo in his tracks.

"OF COURSE NOT! PABLO IS OUR FRIEND! WE DON'T EAT FRIENDS," said Tere.

Pablo ignored the fact that she had said friends and not mice in general.

"Wow, you all are really cute!" said Pablo.

"We know," said all three kittens.

"What about the flute music that lured Ugly Cat out here?" asked Big Mike.

"OH, THAT. IT'S AN OLD MUSIC BOX THAT WE TURN ON FOR THE KITTENS. IT HELPS THEM GO TO SLEEP," said Tamarindo. He walked over to a music box and turned it on. The music that

they had heard back in the kitchen resounded
in the grotto.

"If the music box was the
source of the sound, then why
did you seem like you were in
a trance?" Pablo asked Ugly Cat.

"I WASN'T IN A TRANCE, PABLO, I WAS JUST MOVED BY THE BEAUTY OF THE MUSIC," Ugly Cat said. "AND YOU WERE RIGHT, THERE ARE NO SUCH THINGS AS CHANEQUES. JUST LIKE THERE ARE NO SUCH THINGS AS GHOSTS."

As Ugly Cat said that, thunder roared above them, and scratching and hissing and wailing were heard at the entrance of the grotto. Then a shrieking, shivering, terrifying voice rang out.

"Paaaaabbloooooo . . . I'm here for you. I'm here for aaaall of youuuuuuu!"

CHAPTER NINE

Home Again/
A La Casita

Everybody screamed of course.

"Oh, cielos!" Pablo called out. "A ghost! A ghost!"

"I can't breathe! It's sucking the life out of me! I feel it!" screamed Big Mike in a panic.

"THE KITTENS! COVER THE KITTENS!" instructed Ugly Cat.

Everyone in the grotto panicked. Well, mostly they were just running from one side of the grotto to the other. None of them wanted to be near the ghost or where they heard the ghost's voice.

Then they heard someone cackling.

"OH MY GALLETAS! THE GHOST iS MOCKiNG US!" Ugly Cat said angrily.

Then . . . laughter. Not cackling, not frightening, just laughter.

"Wait a minute," said Big Mike. "I know that beautiful laugh anywhere! Cleopatra! Cleopatra! Come out from wherever you're hiding!"

Before she showed her face, the group could hear the click-clacking of Cleopatra's perfectly painted nails on the grotto floor. She was still laughing when she came in.

"Oh man," Cleopatra started, and then fell on the floor laughing, hardly able to get a word out. "Okay . . . okay . . . ba-ha-ha-ha . . . I . . . just . . . can't . . . stop . . . laughing . . . ha-ha-ha-ha!" She rolled over holding her stomach from laughing so hard.

"Why would you do that?!" exclaimed Pablo.

"YEAH! POR QUÉ?" asked Ugly Cat.

"Whew." Cleopatra sighed and sat up. "Why, Pablo? Why you ask? Why would I have followed you and scared you into dropping chili cheese fries?"

"That was you?" Pablo's eyes opened wide.

"Of course it was me," answered Cleopatra, rolling her eyes. "The answer to why I would do that, Pablo, is easy. I mean, how could you eat my elote? How?"

Everyone groaned.

"NOT THIS AGAIN," said Tamarindo.

"Y SIGUE CON EL ELOTE! HOLY GUACAMOLE. LET IT GO, CLEOPATRA!" said Ugly Cat.

"Let it go? I can't let it go! I wanted that elote so bad," said Cleopatra. "I can still taste it." She closed her eyes and pretended to eat something and licked her lips. "You took that away from me, Pablo. You did. And that's why I scared you."

"I cannot believe that you would scare all of us, even innocent kittens, because of a thing that happened so long ago, and that was an accident to top it off," Pablo said, shaking his head.

Tere nodded her head. And so did the kittens.

"Well, maybe I did take it a little too far," Cleopatra said. "I'm sorry, kittens. I'm sorry, everyone else but Pablo."

"Argh! Look, I'll find you another elote! I'll bring it to you! Extra queso, even, if we can just be friends again," Pablo implored.

Cleopatra thought about it. "Okay. When you bring me that elote, I'll consider a truce. It doesn't mean that we're not friends, just that I won't believe it until I eat it."

"Okay, fine. Now look we

need to go home. Tamarindo, your family misses you. Kai and Ronin, your humans, really miss you."

"I KNOW, BUT I STILL WANT TO HELP TERE," said Tamarindo.

"TAMARINDO," Tere said, smiling, "YOU'VE DONE ENOUGH. I'LL BE FINE HERE. WE'LL BE FINE HERE. THE NEW OWNERS OF THE HOUSE WILL MOVE IN SOON, AND UNTIL THEN, SOME OF THE TEENAGERS WHO HANG OUT AT THE POOL AND PLAY SOCCER IN THE BACKYARD BRING ME FOOD AND WATER. WHEN THE OWNERS MOVE IN, HOPEFULLY THEY'LL LET US STAY AROUND HERE; IF NOT, I HEARD ONE OF ONE OF THE TEENAGERS SAY THEY WANTED TO TAKE US HOME."

"ARE YOU SURE?" asked Tamarindo.

"OF COURSE. GO BACK TO YOUR FAMILY. YOUR HUMAN FAMILY," said Tere. "TELL YOUR TÍOS FEO Y TAMARINDO BYE-BYE, KITTENS."

"Bye-bye, Tíos! Come back to see us soon," said the kittens in their small kitten voices.

"**Without the mean doggy,**" the smallest kitten added, glaring at Cleopatra.

"Ouch," she said. "I guess I deserve that. I promise, kitties, next time I come by I won't scare you."

"**Promise?**" asked the little one.

"Promise," said Cleopatra.

"**WELL, WE SHOULD BE GOING,**" said Ugly Cat.

Everyone had to give everyone a kiss on the cheek and had to say good-bye to everyone else, so it took them a long time to leave. As they were walking out of the grotto, Pablo took out a piece of something from his pocket and slurped it down.

"**YOU STILL HAVE LEFTOVER SAND-WICH?**" Ugly Cat shook his head.

"Oh, no, this is a piece of leche flan that I snagged from Tamarindo's house," Pablo said, spitting sweet caramel sauce as he spoke.

"**LECHE FLAN?!**" exclaimed Tamarindo. "**THEY REALLY DO MISS ME! LECHE FLAN IS MY FAVORITE SNACK! WE NEED TO HURRY BEFORE IT'S ALL GONE!**"

Pablo shoved the last piece of the sweet in his mouth, and the group took off running and skipping back to the Aquinos' house. They splashed and laughed and got muddy.

Mostly they talked about all the delicious food they would eat that evening because the Aquinos would be so happy that Tamarindo was back.

But more than excited about the food they were going to eat, Ugly Cat and his best friend, Pablo, were excited that they had found Tamarindo.

"I AM SO GLAD THAT TAMARINDO WASN'T REALLY MISSING," said Ugly Cat.

"Me, too," added Pablo.

"I AM ESPECIALLY GLAD THAT IT WASN'T A CHANEQUES-RELATED SITUATION AFTER ALL," Ugly Cat added, looking relieved.

"You're still going on about the chaneques?" groaned Cleopatra.

"Hey, it could have happened!" Pablo said, because while he didn't believe 100 percent in chaneques, Ugly was his best friend and friends always stuck together.

Cleopatra rolled her eyes at Pablo and then

trotted ahead with Big Mike and Tamarindo, who were talking and laughing about how the cockroaches had scared the teenagers.

"GRACIAS, PABLO," Ugly said, putting a paw on his best friend's shoulder. "YOU'RE A GOOD FRIEND."

"Sometimes I think we're more than friends," said Pablo. "Sometimes I think we're like family."

"I THINK YOU'RE RIGHT," Ugly said, smiling.

Pablo patted the paw that was still on his shoulder.

"WAIT, DO YOU HEAR THAT?" asked Ugly, eyes as round as cheese pizzas.

"The softly playing flute music that seems to be coming from nowhere?" responded Pablo.

"YEAH," said Ugly.

"Nope. But we should walk faster," said Pablo.

And after a long day, filled with ghosts, chaneques, and lost and found brothers, the two best friends, who were more like family, quickly caught up with the group ahead and hurried home.

Inside the Old Herrera house, Lenny and George and the other cockroaches put down the flute they'd found in the closet and laughed until their stomachs hurt.

FIN

GLOSSARY

A la casita: To our little home

A ver: Let's see

Abrigo: Coat

Albóndigas: Mexican meatball soup

Amigo: Friend

Así no más: Just like that

Baba: Drool

Bistek Tagalog: Meat dish originally from the Philippines

Carne asada: Grilled meat and also a barbecue

Chaneque: A mythological troll-like being in Mexican folklore that lures children with flute music

Cielos: Heavens

Chicle: Gum

Chonies: Slang for underwear

Cucarachas/cucarachitas: Cockroaches/ little cockroaches

Elotes: Corn on the cob with cotija cheese and chili

Empanada: A type of turnover

Fantasma: Ghost

Feo: Ugly

Galletas: Cookies

Gallina: Chicken

Hermanito: Little brother; can mean little as in size or as in younger in age; can also be a term of endearment for a brother

Hermano: Brother

Juan Gabriel: Legendary Mexican singer who passed away in 2016

La Llorona: Ghost woman in Mexican folklore

Leche flan: A dessert dish made with milk and eggs

Lo agarré de la cola: I grabbed it by the tail

Lumpia: Spring roll of Chinese origin, a common appetizer in the Philippines

Mayonesa: Mayonnaise

Mira: Look

Miré un fantasma: I saw a ghost

Por qué?: Why?

Pupusa: Traditional Salvadoran dish of a thick corn tortilla often stuffed with a filling of cheese or meat

Qué delicioso: How delicious

Qué te pasa: What's happening to you? or What's wrong with you?

Querido: Dear

Queso de rancho: Artisanal cheese that is made on a ranch

Te digo: I tell you

Tíos: Uncles

Torta de huevo: Egg sandwich

Tu no sabes nada: You don't know anything

Turon: A snack popular in the Philippines made of bananas and jackfruit rolled in a spring roll

Un ojo de agua: Water hole

Vamos a ver en donde anda tu hermano:
Let's go see where your brother is

Y luego: And then

Y sigue con el elote: And there she goes on
again about the corn

Y sopatelas: And wham

RECIPE

WANT TO MAKE YOUR OWN LECHE FLAN?

Try this recipe at home.

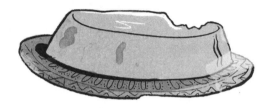

Yields: 10 servings

Supplies needed:

One 9- or 10-inch round baking dish

Small saucepan

Aluminum foil

Large roasting pan

Cheesecloth

A parent or guardian

Ingredients:

½ cup granulated sugar

12 egg yolks

1 can (14 ounces) sweetened condensed milk

1 can (12 ounces) evaporated milk

1 teaspoon vanilla extract

Directions:

1. Preheat oven to 375 degrees F (175 degrees C).

2. Over medium-low heat, melt sugar in a small, heavy saucepan, stirring continuously until it becomes a golden caramel. Remove from heat and pour into a 9- or 10-inch baking dish, tilting to cover bottom of mold. Set aside to cool.

3. In a large bowl, gently stir together egg yolks, evaporated milk, condensed milk, and vanilla until smooth. Using a cheesecloth, strain mixture into caramel-coated baking dish.

4. Cover baking dish with aluminum foil and set in the middle of a large roasting pan, before placing pan on oven rack. Pour boiling water into roasting pan until it covers half of the baking dish (about 1 inch of water).

5. Bake in preheated oven for about 50 to 60 minutes, until center is just set. Remove from oven and allow to cool for one hour before chilling overnight in the refrigerator. To remove from the baking dish, slide a knife around the edges of the pan and flip over onto a rimmed serving plate.

6. Comer con gusto!

ABOUT THE AUTHOR

Isabel Quintero is the daughter of Mexican immigrants. She lives and writes in the Inland Empire of Southern California, where she was born and raised. Her debut novel, *Gabi, A Girl in Pieces*, was the recipient of five starred reviews and several awards, including the 2015 William C. Morris YA Debut Award and the Tomás Rivera Mexican American Children's Book Award. Of her first chapter book, *Ugly Cat & Pablo*, *Kirkus Reviews* said, "Both chapter-book and reluctant readers will go for this one like cats to paletas." For fun, Isabel likes to read, write, and embarrass her younger brother by dancing in public.

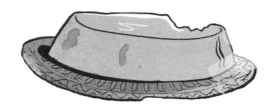

ABOUT THE
ILLUSTRATOR

Tom Knight lives on Mersea Island on the
Essex coast of England. He was raised on a
steady diet of Beano comics, Tintin books, and
good sea air.

ACKNOWLEDGMENTS

I want to thank Scholastic for giving me the opportunity to bring these two very best friends to life. Thanks to Nancy Mercado for reaching out to me (I seriously was like, "Whaaat?!") and for her careful eye and all the patience in the world. Thanks to Peter Steinberg, my agent, and the whole Foundry team, and also to Erika Wurth for making sure that he and I met. Thank you to Tom Knight for imagining Ugly Cat and Pablo almost exactly as I did. A huge thank-you to Claudia Guzman for being the first to read Ugly Cat and Pablo and the first teacher to let them in her classroom. As always, thank you to all my friends and family for all your support. Thank you to Fernando and the familia Flores for teaching me about chaneques. Big thanks and love to the real Kai and Ronin, and to their parents, especially their mom, Chrysta, one of the bestest friends a person could ever want. Gracias a mis padres y a mi hermano quienes siempre me apoyan, los quiero mucho. Thanks to my sister-in-law, Amanda, for her support. And lastly, thank you to all the readers and librarians who continue to support me—I am forever in your debt.

ABOUT THE AUTHOR

Isabel Quintero is the daughter of Mexican immigrants. She lives and writes in the Inland Empire of Southern California, where she was born and raised. Of her first chapter book, *Ugly Cat and Pablo*, *Kirkus Reviews* said, "Both chapter-book and reluctant readers will go for this one like cats to paletas." For fun, Isabel likes to read, write, and embarrass her younger brother by dancing in public.

UGLY CAT'S BROTHER, TAMARINDO, IS MISSING!

UGLY CAT and his best friend, Pablo, head over to Tamarindo's house, but he is nowhere to be found. Instead they find a giant spread of delectable food, which *almost* distracts them.

But then a hamster named Peaches gives them a credible lead on where Tamarindo might be. The only problem is that everything is pointing to a well-known haunted casa in the Mariposa Valley neighborhood.

Can **UGLY CAT** and Pablo summon up all their courage and find Tamarindo? Even if it means wrestling ghosts?

■**SCHOLAS**[TIC] t, © 2018 Scholastic Inc.
Cover design by Nina Goffi
www.scholastic.com

APPEALS TO
2ND–4TH GRADERS

READING LEVEL
GRADE 3

More leveling information for this book:
www.scholastic.com/readinglevel

ISBN 978-0-545-94095-5
50699

$6.99 US / $8.99 CAN

9 780545 940955